HANDA'S HEN

EILEEN BROWNE

WALKER BOOKS
AND SUBSIDIARIES

LONDON • BOSTON • SYDNEY • AUCKLAND

Handa's grandma had one black hen.

Her name was Mondi – and every morning

Handa gave Mondi her breakfast.

baby bullfrogs

spoonbills

starlings

For John and Milo

The children featured in this book are from the Luo tribe of south-west Kenya.

*The wild creatures are the Citrus Swallowtail (butterfly), Striped Grass Mouse,
Yellow-headed Dwarf Gecko, Beautiful Sunbird, Armoured Ground Cricket,
(young) African Bullfrog, African Spoonbill and Superb Starling.*

*The author would like to thank everyone who helped her research this book,
in particular Joseph Ngetich from the Agricultural Office of the Kenya High Commission.*

First published 2002 by Walker Books Ltd
87 Vauxhall Walk, London SE11 5HJ

This edition published 2003

18 20 19 17

© 2002 Eileen Browne

The right of Eileen Browne to be identified
as author/illustrator of this work has been asserted by her
in accordance with the Copyright, Designs and Patents Act 1988

This book has been typeset in Garamond Book

Printed in China

British Library Cataloguing in Publication Data:
a catalogue record for this book is available from the British Library

ISBN 978-0-7445-9815-5

www.walker.co.uk

One day, Mondi didn't come for her food.

"Grandma!" called Handa. "Can you see Mondi?"

"No," said Grandma. "But I can see your friend."

"Akeyo!" said Handa. "Help me find Mondi."

Handa and Akeyo hunted round the hen house.

"Look! Two fluttery butterflies," said Akeyo.

"But where's Mondi?" said Handa.

They peered under a grain store.
"Shh! Three stripy mice," said Akeyo.
"But where's Mondi?" said Handa.

They peeped behind some clay pots.

"I can see four little lizards," said Akeyo.

"But where's Mondi?" said Handa.

They searched round some flowering trees.

"Five beautiful sunbirds," said Akeyo.

"But where's Mondi?" said Handa.

They looked in the long, waving grass.

"Six jumpy crickets!" said Akeyo. "Let's catch them."

"I want to find Mondi," said Handa.

They went all the way down to the water hole.
"Baby bullfrogs," said Akeyo. "There are seven!"

"But where's … oh look! Footprints!" said Handa.
They followed the footprints and found...

"Only spoonbills," said Handa. "Seven … no, eight.
But where, oh where is Mondi?"

"I hope she hasn't been swallowed by a spoonbill –
or eaten by a lion," said Akeyo.

Feeling sad, they went back towards Grandma's.
"Nine shiny starlings – over there!" said Akeyo.

"Listen," said Handa.   cheep cheep   "What's that?"

cheep
cheep   cheep cheep   cheep
cheep   cheep

cheep
cheep

"It's coming from under that bush.

Shall we peep?"

Handa, Akeyo, Mondi and ten chicks

hurried and scurried and skipped back to Grandma's ...

where they all had a very late breakfast.

hen

mice

lizards

sunbirds

crickets

butterflies

baby bullfrogs

spoonbills

starlings

chicks

Look out for:

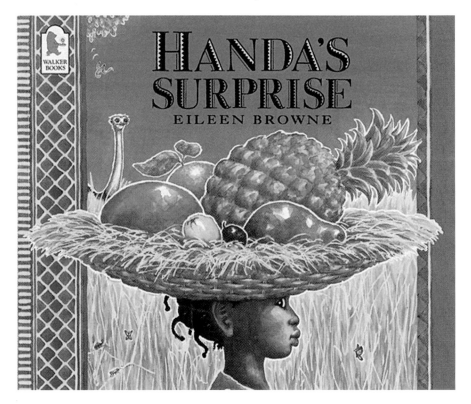

ISBN 978-0-7445-3634-8

"So luscious it seems almost edible." – *Observer*

"Rich, hot colours and fluid brush-strokes zap each scene into life." – *Independent*

A *Guardian* 'Diverse Voices' selection: one of the 50 best culturally diverse children's books.

Available from all good booksellers

www.walker.co.uk